PANDA GIGANTE
Ailuropoda melanoleuca
China

Los osos panda viven en las montañas del centro de China. Su dieta es 99% bambú.

OSO POLAR
Ursus maritimus
Círculo Ártico

Los osos polares son los osos más grandes del mundo. La mayoría vive dentro del Círculo Ártico.

OSO NEGRO
Ursus americanus
América del Norte

El oso negro es un oso de mediano tamaño que vive en los bosques de América del Norte.

GIANT PANDA
Ailuropoda melanoleuca
China

Panda bears live in the mountains of central China. The Panda bear's diet is 99% bamboo.

POLAR BEAR
Ursus maritimus
Arctic Circle

Polar bears are the world's largest bears. Most live within the Arctic Circle.

BLACK BEAR
Ursus americanus
North America

The black bear is a medium-sized bear that lives in the forests of North America.

OSO DE PELUCHE
Oso honorario
En todo el mundo

El oso de peluche es un oso de juguete. En inglés se le llama "Teddy bear" por un presidente de EE.UU. llamado Theodore "Teddy" Roosevelt.

OSO PARDO
Ursus arctos
Europa, Asia y América del Norte

Los osos pardos son los osos más comunes. Se encuentran por toda América del Norte, Europa y Asia.

OSO MALAYO
Helarctos malayanus
Sureste de Asia

El oso malayo es el oso más pequeño del mundo. También se le llama "oso de los cocoteros" por su afición a estos frutos y "oso del sol".

koala

TEDDY BEAR
Honorary 'Bear'
Worldwide

The Teddy bear is a stuffed toy bear named after the US president Theodore Roosevelt whose nickname was Teddy.

BROWN BEAR
Ursus arctos
Europe, Asia and North America

Brown bears are the most common of all bears. They can be found all over North America, Europe and Asia.

SUN BEAR
Helarctos malayanus
Southeast Asia

The sun bear is the world's smallest bear. The sun bear is also known as a honey bear because it loves to eat honey.

Para Emily y Jessica

For Emily and Jessica

First published in English by Fremantle Press, Australia, in 2010.

Bilingual Spanish/English edition first published in the United States of
America in 2013 by Star Bright Books. Inc. The name Star Bright Books and
the Star Bright Books logo are registered trademarks of Star Bright Books, Inc.
Please visit: www.starbrightbooks.com. For bulk orders, please email:
orders@starbrightbooks.com, or call customer service at: (617) 354-1300.

Spanish/English Hardback ISBN-13: 978-1-59572-644-5
Star Bright Books / MA / 00107130
Printed in China (C&C) 10 9 8 7 6 5 4 3 2 1

Spanish/English Paperback ISBN-13: 978-1-59572-645-2
Star Bright Books / MA / 00107130
Printed in China (C&C) 10 9 8 7 6 5 4 3 2 1

Translated by Eida Del Risco

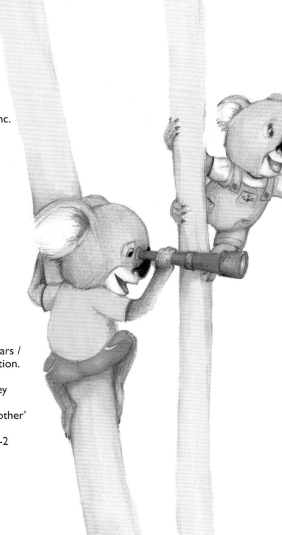

Library of Congress Cataloging-in-Publication Data

Thompson, Michael, 1977- author , illustrator.
 Los otros osos / escrito e ilustrado por Michael Thompson = The other bears /
written and illustrated by Michael Thompson. -- Spanish/English bilingual edition.
     pages cm
 Summary:"Mother and Father Koala are suspicious of the 'other' bears. They
don't like the panda bears and they don't trust the polar bears. But their
grumpiness melts away as they watch their little Koalas play together with 'other'
bears"-- Provided by publisher.
 ISBN 978-1-59572-644-5 (hardcover : alk. paper) -- ISBN 978-1-59572-645-2
(pbk. : alk. paper)
 [1. Koala--Fiction. 2. Bears--Fiction. 3. Toleration--Fiction. 4. Spanish language
materials--Bilingual.] I. Title. II. Title: Other bears.
 PZ73.T48 2013
 [E]--dc23
                        2013021805

Los otros osos

The Other Bears

Por/By Michael Thompson

Star Bright Books
Cambridge, Massachusetts

A los koalas les gusta
que les digan "osos".

Koalas just LOVE to
be called koala bears.

Pero vaya sorpresa que se llevaron,

cuando los *otros* osos llegaron.

But they were in for a big surprise

when the *other* bears arrived.

Primero llegaron los osos panda.

First came the panda bears.

—No me gustan sus orejas —gruñó Papá Koala.

—Ni sus zapatos —rezongó Mamá Koala.

—Pues a nosotros nos encanta su comida —dijeron los
koalitas con una sonrisa.

"I don't like their ears," grumbled Father Koala.

"Or their shoes," griped Mother Koala.

"But we love their food," grinned the little koalas.

Luego llegaron los osos polares.

Next came the polar bears.

—No me gustan sus garras —refunfuñó Papá Koala.

—Ni sus abrigos —se indignó Mamá Koala.

"I don't like their claws," growled Father Koala.

"Or their coats," groaned Mother Koala.

—Pues a nosotros nos encantan sus chistes
—dijeron los koalitas riéndose.

"But we love their jokes,"
giggled the little koalas.

Después llegaron los osos negros.

Third came the black bears.

—No me gusta el ruido que hacen —se lamentó Papá Koala.

—Ni sus uniformes — se quejó Mamá Koala.

—Pues a nosotros nos encantan sus canciones —dijeron

alegres los koalitas.

"I don't like their noise," wailed Father Koala.

"Or their uniforms," whined Mother Koala.

"But we love their songs," whooped the little koalas.

Entonces llegaron los osos pardos.

Then came the brown bears.

—No me gustan sus dientes —protestó Papá Koala.

—Ni ese gorro —suspiró Mamá Koala.

—Pues a nosotros nos encantan sus cuentos

—dijeron los koalitas.

"I don't like their teeth," snapped Father Koala.

"Or that hat," sniffed Mother Koala.

"But we love their stories," said the little koalas.

Por último llegaron los osos malayos.

Last came the sun bears.

—No me gustan sus bicicletas —bufó Papá Koala.

—Ni sus sombrillas — resopló Mamá Koala.

"I don't like their bicycles," huffed Father Koala.

"Or their umbrellas," puffed Mother Koala.

—Pues a nosotros nos encantan sus juegos
—dijeron los koalitas riéndose.

"But we love their games," laughed the little koalas.

Papá Koala y Mamá Koala estaban tan
malhumorados que ya no podían disfrutar nada.

Pero entonces sucedió que...

Father Koala and Mother Koala
were becoming so grumpy
they didn't seem to like anything anymore.

But then . . .

Todo su malhumor se lo llevó el viento,

All their grumpiness melted away,

cuando vieron a sus koalitas jugar contentos.

watching the little koalas play.

Porque cada oso era aún más feliz,

For each was a happier little bear,

ahora que los otros osos estaban ahí.

now that the other bears were there.

KOALA
Phascolarctos cinereus
Este y sur de Australia

Los koalas no son osos de verdad, sino marsupiales, que son animales que cargan a sus bebés en una bolsa. Los koalas comen más que nada hojas de eucalipto y duermen cerca de 16 horas al día.

KOALA
Phascolarctos cinereus
Eastern and Southern Australia

Koalas are not really bears. They are marsupials, animals that carry their babies in a pouch. Koalas eat mostly eucalyptus leaves, and they sleep for about 16 hours a day.

OSO DE ANTEOJOS
Tremarctos ornatus
América del Sur

Los osos de anteojos son los únicos osos de América del Sur. También se les llama osos andinos porque viven en los Andes y alrededores.

OSO PEREZOSO
Melursus ursinus
Asia

Los osos perezosos tienen una capa de pelo largo y negro y comen frutas e insectos. Casi todos viven en la India y Sri Lanka. Son los únicos osos que llevan sus crías a la espalda.

OSO TIBETANO
Ursus thibetanus
Asia

Al oso tibetano también se le llama oso de la luna por el trozo de pelaje blanco en forma de luna que tiene en el pecho.

SPECTACLED BEAR
Tremarctos ornatus
South America

Spectacled bears are the only bears from South America. They are also known as Andean bears because they live in and around the Andes mountains.

SLOTH BEAR
Melursus ursinus
Asia

Sloth bears have shaggy black hair and eat fruit and insects. Most live in India and Sri Lanka. They're the only bears that carry their babies on their backs.

ASIAN BLACK BEAR
Ursus thibetanus
Asia

The Asian black bear is also known as a moon bear because of the moon shaped patch of white fur on its chest.